A Cretaceous

Dinosaur Cove™

March of the
Armoured Beasts

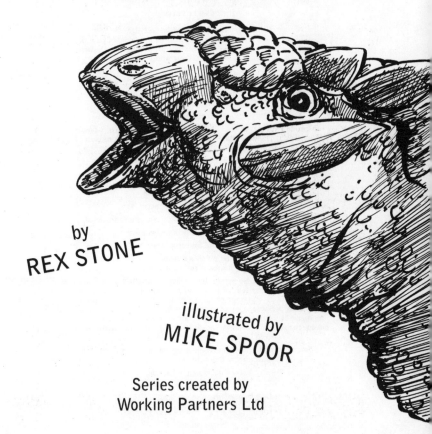

by
REX STONE

illustrated by
MIKE SPOOR

Series created by
Working Partners Ltd

OXFORD
UNIVERSITY PRESS

With special thanks to Jane Clarke

To all my SCBWI friends

OXFORD
UNIVERSITY PRESS

Great Clarendon Street, Oxford OX2 6DP
Oxford University Press is a department of the University of Oxford.
It furthers the University's objective of excellence in research, scholarship,
and education by publishing worldwide in

Oxford   New York

Auckland   Cape Town   Dar es Salaam   Hong Kong   Karachi
Kuala Lumpur   Madrid   Melbourne   Mexico City   Nairobi
New Delhi   Shanghai   Taipei   Toronto

With offices in

Argentina   Austria   Brazil   Chile   Czech Republic   France   Greece
Guatemala   Hungary   Italy   Japan   Poland   Portugal   Singapore
South Korea   Switzerland   Thailand   Turkey   Ukraine   Vietnam

Oxford is a registered trade mark of Oxford University Press
in the UK and in certain other countries

© Working Partners Limited 2008
Illustrations © Mike Spoor 2008

Series created by Working Partners Ltd

Dinosaur Cove is a registered trademark of Working Partners Ltd

The moral rights of the author have been asserted

Database right Oxford University Press (maker)

First published 2008
First published in this edition 2013

British Library Cataloguing in Publication Data

Data available

ISBN: 978-0-19-279367-6

1 3 5 7 9 10 8 6 4 2

Printed in Italy

Paper used in the production of this book is a natural,
recyclable product made from wood grown in sustainable forests
The manufacturing process conforms to the environmental
regulations of the country of origin

FACT FILE

➡️ JAMIE HAS JUST MOVED FROM THE CITY TO LIVE IN THE LIGHTHOUSE IN DINOSAUR COVE. JAMIE'S DAD IS OPENING A DINOSAUR MUSEUM ON THE BOTTOM FLOOR OF THE LIGHTHOUSE. WHEN JAMIE GOES HUNTING FOR FOSSILS IN THE CRUMBLING CLIFFS ON THE BEACH HE MEETS A LOCAL BOY, TOM, AND THE TWO DISCOVER AN AMAZING SECRET: A WORLD WITH **REAL, LIVE DINOSAURS!** TRACKING DINOSAURS IS EXCITING, BUT DANGER SURROUNDS THE BOYS AT EVERY TURN.

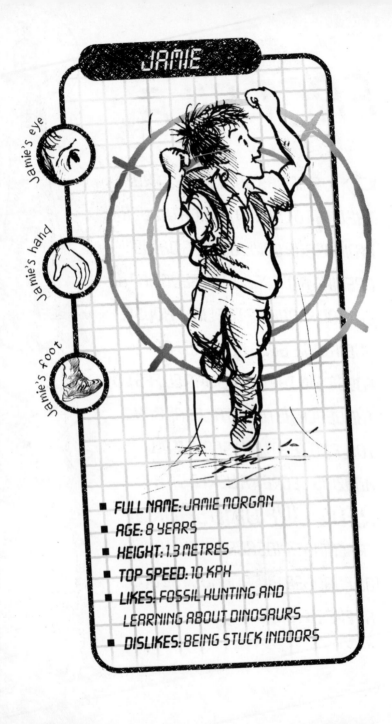

JAMIE

Jamie's eye

Jamie's hand

Jamie's foot

- **FULL NAME:** JAMIE MORGAN
- **AGE:** 8 YEARS
- **HEIGHT:** 1.3 METRES
- **TOP SPEED:** 10 KPH
- **LIKES:** FOSSIL HUNTING AND LEARNING ABOUT DINOSAURS
- **DISLIKES:** BEING STUCK INDOORS

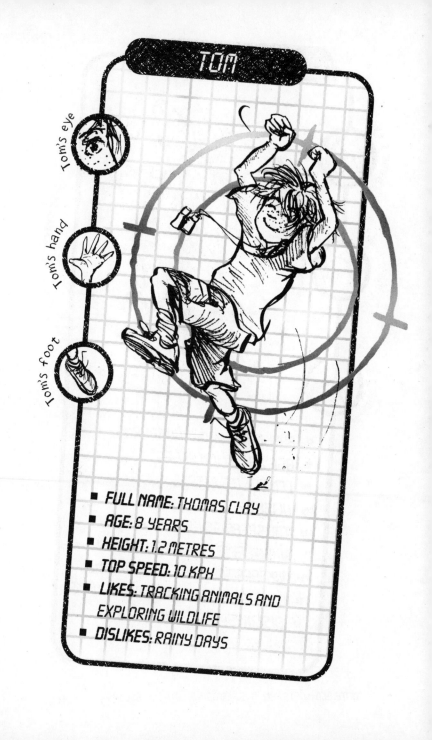

Tom's eye

Tom's hand

Tom's foot

TOM

- **FULL NAME:** THOMAS CLAY
- **AGE:** 8 YEARS
- **HEIGHT:** 1.2 METRES
- **TOP SPEED:** 10 KPH
- **LIKES:** TRACKING ANIMALS AND EXPLORING WILDLIFE
- **DISLIKES:** RAINY DAYS

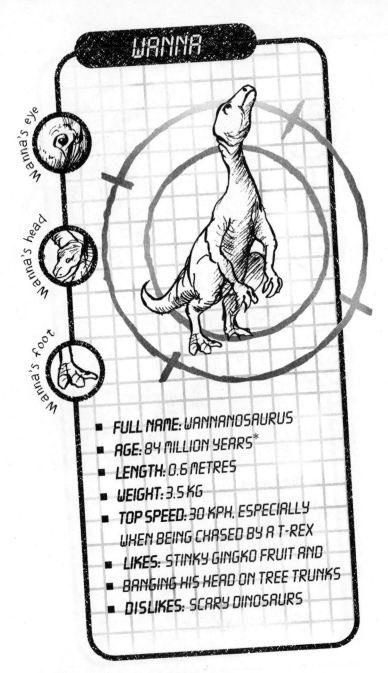

WANNA

Wanna's eye
Wanna's head
Wanna's foot

- **FULL NAME:** WANNANOSAURUS
- **AGE:** 84 MILLION YEARS*
- **LENGTH:** 0.6 METRES
- **WEIGHT:** 3.5 KG
- **TOP SPEED:** 30 KPH, ESPECIALLY WHEN BEING CHASED BY A T-REX
- **LIKES:** STINKY GINGKO FRUIT AND
- BANGING HIS HEAD ON TREE TRUNKS
- **DISLIKES:** SCARY DINOSAURS

*NOTE: SCIENTISTS CALL THIS PERIOD THE LATE CRETACEOUS

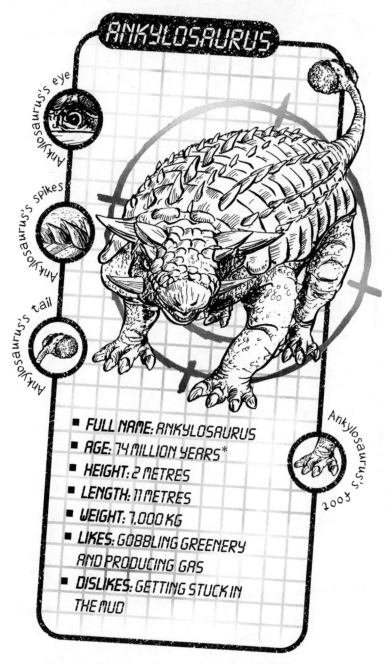

ANKYLOSAURUS

Ankylosaurus's eye

Ankylosaurus's spikes

Ankylosaurus's tail

Ankylosaurus's foot

- **FULL NAME:** ANKYLOSAURUS
- **AGE:** 74 MILLION YEARS*
- **HEIGHT:** 2 METRES
- **LENGTH:** 11 METRES
- **WEIGHT:** 7,000 KG
- **LIKES:** GOBBLING GREENERY AND PRODUCING GAS
- **DISLIKES:** GETTING STUCK IN THE MUD

*NOTE: SCIENTISTS CALL THIS PERIOD THE LATE CRETACEOUS

DINOSAUR COVE

Village

Marina

Sealight Head

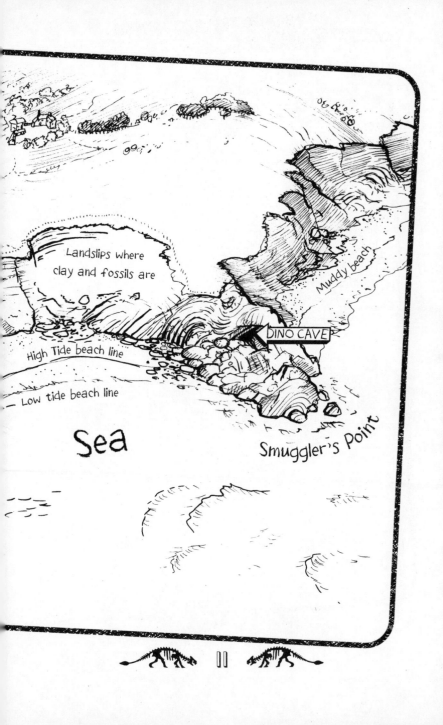

Landslips where clay and fossils are

Muddy beach

DINO CAVE

High Tide beach line

Low tide beach line

Sea

Smuggler's Point

Jamie picked out a small fossil
from the heap of gooey mud that
had slipped down onto Dinosaur
Cove beach in the night. The stone
looked like a stubby pencil with
a sharp point. He wiped it on his

13

jeans and handed it to his best friend Tom.

'That could be a dinosaur tooth,' Jamie's grandad said, putting down his fishing bucket and leaning in for a closer look.

'It's not a dinosaur tooth,' Tom replied. 'They don't look anything like this in real li—'

Jamie nudged Tom with his elbow. Grandad didn't know they'd discovered real

live dinosaurs through a secret cave
in Dinosaur Cove.

'Let's find out what it is.' Jamie
rummaged inside his backpack.
'Compass . . . cheese and pickle
sandwiches . . . Fossil Finder!' Jamie
flipped open the lid of the hand-held
computer and typed 'stubby pencil' in
the search box. At once a picture of
the fossil popped up.

'*BEL-EM-NITE*,' he read. '*THIS
BULLET-SHAPED FOSSIL IS THE BODY
OF A SEA CREATURE LIKE A SQUID.*'
Jamie snapped the Fossil Finder shut
and put it, and the belemnite, in his
backpack.

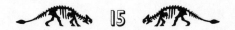

'Fossil squid, eh?' Grandad chuckled. 'You can't eat those! I'm off to find some *fresh* fish.'

'And we should go find some fresh dinosaurs,' Tom whispered to Jamie as Grandad gathered up his fishing gear.

'Don't get stuck in the mud!' Grandad's eyes twinkled as he turned towards the sea. 'It'll swallow you up and spit out your bones, just like it did to the dinosaurs . . . '

The instant Grandad was out of hearing range, the boys yelled, 'Dino World here we come!'

They dashed towards the path that led from the beach up to the

smugglers' cave where the hidden
entrance to Dino World was. At the
bottom of the path, Jamie spotted
two large footprints in the sand.

Jamie skidded to a halt. 'Wait,
Tom. Someone has been here!'

Tom bent down to
examine the shoe
imprints. 'They're fresh,'
he said, 'and they're
leading up our
path!'

'Oh no,' Jamie
groaned.
'What if
someone's

found the way through our cave into
Dino World?'

'Then it wouldn't be our secret
any more,' Tom said grimly. 'You
know grown-ups. They'd sell tickets
to visitors to make money out of it.'

Jamie frowned. 'Or they'd say
it was dangerous and

close it up completely. We might never get to go back!'

Jamie and Tom examined the ground carefully and followed the footprints up

the steep slope to the pile of boulders beneath their secret cave.

'Someone definitely came this way,' Jamie said.

'We've got to make sure the cave's safe.' He clambered up the boulders as fast as he could.

19

'What are you waiting for?'
he called from the top. Tom was
lingering over a footprint beneath the
boulders. Jamie hopped impatiently
from one foot to another as Tom
scaled the boulders and hauled
himself up next to Jamie.

'There's no need to panic.' Tom
grinned and led the way into the cool
cave. 'No one came in here. Those
footprints went on past the boulders.
Our cave is safe!'

'But what if they come back?'
Jamie flicked on his torch and
shone it into the corner of the cave.
The light disappeared into the gap

they'd discovered on their first visit.

'Stop worrying,' Tom told him. 'There's no way someone with feet that big could get through here.'

'You're right.' Jamie breathed a sigh of relief as he pushed his backpack through the tiny gap and crawled in after it, followed closely by Tom.

He flashed his torch over the floor of the secret chamber and picked out the fossilized footprints of

their
dinosaur
friend,
Wanna, which
had led them twice
into Dino World.

'That foot wouldn't fit in these tracks, either.' Jamie stepped into the first of the small clover-shaped prints in the solid rock. 'But they're exactly the right size for us!'

'Then let's track dinosaurs!' Tom declared. 'I'm right behind you.'

'One . . . two . . . three . . . ' Jamie's heart beat faster as he counted each

step. *What kind of dinosaurs will we see today?* he wondered.

'. . . four . . .'

The cave wall in front of him looked like solid rock, but as he put his foot forward a crack of light appeared.

'FIVE!'

The crack of light widened and the ground felt soft under Jamie's trainers as he stepped from the dark cave into Dino World.

Jamie stood blinking in the sunlight
as the familiar smells of wet leaves
and stinky gingko fruit filled his
nose. A moment later, Tom was
standing next to him on Gingko Hill.

'Wanna! Here, Wanna!' Jamie raised his voice above the buzzing insects and the calls of creatures in the steamy jungle.

'That's strange,' Tom said. 'He usually comes right away.'

'Maybe we could track him,' Jamie wondered aloud.

Jamie and Tom examined the ground outside the cave for traces of their faithful dinosaur friend and saw fresh footprints—just like the fossilized ones back in the cave—leading down the side of Gingko Hill.

'Wanna's gone south, down the hill,' Tom said, looking at his compass. 'We've never been that way before. Let's follow him!'

'Hang on a minute.' Jamie picked some smelly gingko fruit and put them in his backpack. 'For Wanna when we see him.'

Then the boys hurried down the hill.

'This is steep!' Jamie said as his legs picked up speed.

'Beat you to the bottom!' Tom yelled.

Jamie raced his friend down the hill, skidding and sliding, grabbing at trailing vines and low branches to keep from falling head over heels.

Jamie leaped down the last little
way to land in the soft mud at the
base of the hill.

Splat!

'I was first!' puffed Jamie as mud
slopped over the top of his trainers.

'No, I was first!' gasped Tom.
A glob of mud plopped off his curly
red hair and splattered onto his
freckly nose.

They looked at each other and
laughed.

'Shh!' said Tom. 'I can hear a
squishing noise.'

Jamie listened for a moment
and then whirled round as a wet,
sandpapery tongue licked his cheek.

'Yuck!' he yelled.

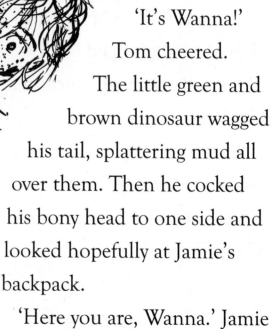

'It's Wanna!'
Tom cheered.
The little green and
brown dinosaur wagged
his tail, splattering mud all
over them. Then he cocked
his bony head to one side and
looked hopefully at Jamie's
backpack.

'Here you are, Wanna.' Jamie
handed Wanna a stinky gingko fruit.
The little dinosaur grunked
happily as he gobbled up the fruit,
then he bounded up to Tom.

'Urgh, stinko breath! Aargh!'
Tom landed on his back in the mud

with Wanna on top of him, licking his face.

The mud squelched as Tom wrestled with Wanna. Jamie looked at the ground more closely. It was churned up and rutted as far as he could see.

'Stop mucking about!' he told
Tom. 'We're standing in the middle
of a dinosaur trackway.'

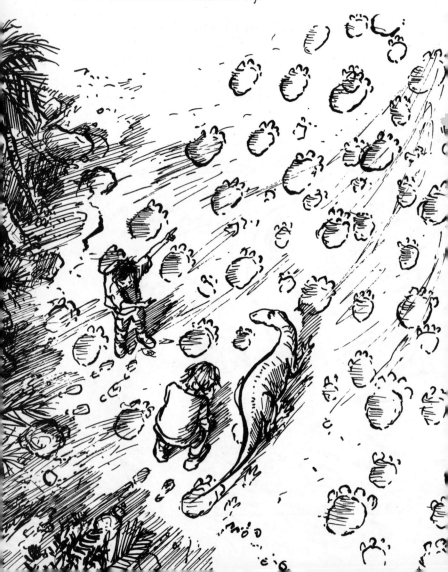

'What do you mean?' Tom asked, disentangling himself from Wanna. 'Look at all these footprints. A group of big, heavy dinosaurs have made this path.' Jamie pointed to a clear footprint at the edge of the track. He stepped on the mud next to it. The dinosaur footprint was over twice as long and much, much deeper than his.

Jamie and Tom bent down and looked carefully at the print. There were four bumps for toes at the front.

'They're all heading that way.' Jamie pointed the way the toes were facing.

Tom wiped his muddy face with the sleeve of his T-shirt. 'Let's track them!'

'Definitely,' agreed Jamie.

They trudged off along the muddy
trackway with Wanna squishing
along beside them. Suddenly, Wanna
froze, his tail sticking out straight
behind him.

The boys stopped and listened.
For a moment there was silence, and
then strange dinosaur calls began to
boom down the trackway.

Aroop! Aroop! Aroooop!

'They sound like foghorns!' Jamie shuddered as the creepy calls echoed around them. Chills were running up and down his spine.

'Are we sure we want to catch up with those dinosaurs?' Tom asked nervously. 'What if they're meat eaters?'

'Good point.' Jamie wiped his muddy hands on his T-shirt, and took the Fossil Finder out of his backpack. He flipped it open and tapped in: *DINOSAUR TRACKS, FOUR TOES.*

'*FOSSIL FOOTPRINTS ARE RARER THAN FOSSIL BONES,*' he read.

'ROUNDED FOOTPRINTS WITH FOUR TOE
MARKS AT THE FRONT WERE MADE BY
HEAVY PLANT EATERS.'

Tom beamed.

'Dinosaurs here we come!'

CHAPTER 3

As Jamie, Tom, and Wanna followed
the trackway, the trees began to
thin out and the ground got wetter.
Jamie's footsteps sank deeper and
deeper into the mud and a thin fog
drifted around them.

Even though they'd left the jungle behind, the tracks stayed at the same width. 'These dinosaurs are walking in a line,' Tom realized.

'Like elephants in those wildlife documentaries,' Jamie said, as he leapt over a giant purple and orange mushroom.

'How many are there?' Tom asked.

'I can't tell,' Jamie said, as his sodden jeans flapped around his legs. 'They've stomped all over each other's tracks. Maybe a t-rex was chasing them?'

'I don't think so,' Tom said. 'If they were running, we'd see their toes digging into the ground. They're on a steady march.'

'Like an army!' Jamie said, pausing beneath a tree with moss dripping from its twisted branches. He peered through the thickening mist. A fresh, salty, tangy smell filled the foggy air. Wanna took a deep sniff and sneezed.

'This must be a marsh where the river widens out and joins the ocean,' Tom said.

Jamie narrowed his eyes. Strange shapes were moving through the murk like ghosts. Dinosaur calls echoed across the marshland.

'Spooky!' Jamie shuddered.

'It's OK. They're plant eaters, remember?' Tom squelched off into the mist, followed by Wanna. Jamie watched as their footprints filled up with bright green slime the instant they'd made them. He bent down and looked more carefully at the sludgy tracks. A series of puddle footprints that looked like smaller versions of the dinosaur prints they were tracking branched off from the path. He followed them as they zigzagged through the marsh.

'Hey, Tom!' he called.

Tom didn't reply. Jamie peered through the fog. He listened, but all

he could hear were the swarms of
insects and the plopping and gurgling
of the marsh.

'Tom?' he yelled. 'Wanna?'

Jamie swallowed hard; he was all
alone.

At last he heard a familiar noise.

Grunk, grunk!

'Wanna!' Jamie breathed a sigh of
relief.

Wanna bounded out of the mist
and licked Jamie's cheek. Tom
splashed after him.

'Wanna sniffed you out,' he
explained. 'I thought you were tracking
the herd behind me.'

'I was following these baby tracks,' Jamie said, pointing them out to Tom. 'It must have wandered off on its own.'

'Babies should stay close to the adults for protection.' Tom frowned. 'That baby could be easy pickings for a predator. We should help it get back to its herd!'

'In this fog?' Jamie asked. As he spoke, he felt a breeze on his face and the fog tumbled across the marsh, lifting a little. Wanna snuffled happily around the slime pools towards a plant with rubbery-looking leaves and bright yellow flowers the size of dinner plates.

'The bog doesn't worry Wanna,'
Tom said. 'We'll be OK if we're
careful.'

They watched as Wanna grabbed a
flower in his mouth, pulled it off and
chewed it up. Then he bounded back
to the boys with his nose covered in
yellow pollen.

'Tasty?' Jamie asked him.

Wanna wagged his tail.

'Perhaps those flowers tempted the baby away from the herd,' Tom said.

'Let's try and find it,' Jamie said and picked his way across the marsh following the baby footprints, trying to avoid the bright green sludge.

'It definitely came this way.' Tom pointed to a torn up patch of flowers.

As Jamie looked up, he tripped on a rock half-buried in the mud and staggered forwards, sinking up to his shins in a pool of green sludge.

'Urgh! This mud stinks of rotten eggs.' Jamie tried to step back onto

the firmer ground, but his feet
wouldn't move.

Bluurp!

The slime bubbled up to his knees.

'Uh oh,' Jamie said, struggling to
move. 'I'm sinking into the bog!'

CHAPTER 4

Jamie tried again to pull his legs free from the bog, but it didn't help. Now, the mud was up to his thighs.

'Stop moving!' Tom yelled. 'You'll sink even quicker if you thrash around. You've got to lie down!'

Jamie looked down at the liquid mud swirling around his legs. 'You're joking.'

'You have to spread out your body weight,' Tom said urgently. 'It's the only way to get yourself out!'

Jamie took a deep breath and then threw himself flat in the revolting green goo. Slime oozed into his mouth, ears, and nose, but at least he stopped sinking. 'It's working!' he spluttered as he crawled out onto the firm ground by the marsh plant and stood dripping.

'This place is dangerous!' he told Tom. 'We should go back.'

'We can't go back yet,' Tom said.
'Listen!'

Jamie scooped out the slime from his ears. Now he could hear a pitiful wailing echoing across the bog.

Aooo, aooo, aooo!

It was coming from behind a curtain of creepers that hung from the branches of a stunted tree. Jamie and Tom walked carefully towards the sound, jumping over the bright green patches of sinking slime. At the stunted tree, Wanna stopped to munch on another patch of yellow marsh plants.

The boys parted the creepers and saw a dinosaur the size of a small car up to

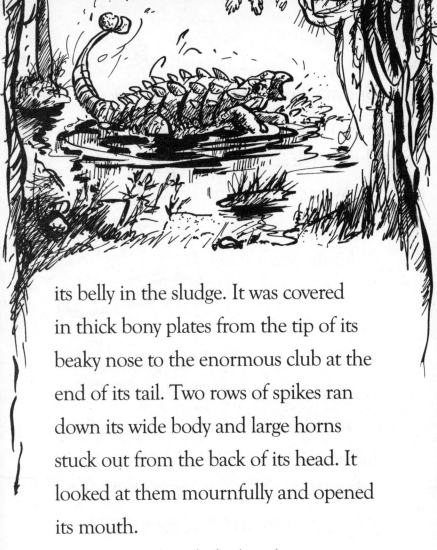

its belly in the sludge. It was covered
in thick bony plates from the tip of its
beaky nose to the enormous club at the
end of its tail. Two rows of spikes ran
down its wide body and large horns
stuck out from the back of its head. It
looked at them mournfully and opened
its mouth.

Aoo-ooo, it wailed, thrashing its
club against the trunk of the tree.

Splinters of rotten wood splattered into the marsh.

'What is it?' Tom asked.

Jamie was already tapping words '*BONY PLATES, SPIKED TAIL*' into the Fossil Finder.

'*AN-KY-LO-SAUR-US*,' he read. '*AN ARMOURED DINOSAUR AS STRONG AS A TANK. THIS SMALL-BRAINED DINOSAUR ATE TOUGH PLANTS AND PROBABLY PRODUCED GREAT QUANTITIES OF GASEOUS WASTE.*'

Jamie snapped the Fossil Finder shut and returned it to his backpack. He looked at the baby dinosaur.

'This anky is small-brained, all right. The more it thrashes its tail, the faster it sinks in the mud!'

'A bit like you, then!' Tom grinned.

Jamie threw a glob of mud at him.

Aooo-oooo! the baby wailed. Wanna started to grunk in sympathy. The anky thumped its tail against the stinky sludge.

'How are we going to get it out?' Jamie sighed.

'We'll have to calm it down first,' Tom said. 'But how do you calm down a dinosaur?'

Jamie looked at Wanna, whose nose was still plastered in pollen. 'Feed it!'

Jamie took a handful of gingko fruit out of his backpack and tossed them, one by one, towards the baby anky. Wanna rushed in and gobbled them up as fast as Jamie could throw them. Then he dashed back to Jamie and stood dribbling and wagging his tail.

'We'll have to try something you don't like!' Jamie rummaged in his

backpack and unwrapped the cheese
and pickle sandwiches Grandad had
made for their lunch. Wanna sneezed
and backed off, shaking his head and
making *gak-gak* noises.

Jamie threw a sandwich under
the baby anky's beak. It stopped
thrashing its tail and sniffed
suspiciously at it. Then it started to
squeal as if it was being poisoned and
began thrashing its tail again.

'Ankies don't like your grandad's
pickle, either!' Tom said.
'What else can we try?'

'The marsh plant!'
Jamie turned back to the

marsh plants and wrenched off three large yellow flower heads. 'One for you, Wanna!'

Wanna pounced on it in delight.

Jamie skimmed the other two across the marsh like a frisbee. The baby dinosaur's long tongue flickered out and pulled a yellow flower into its mouth.

As it chewed, the anky's tail stopped thrashing.

'It's working! Let's get some more flowers.' Jamie bent to pick some more.

'Wait!' Tom said. 'Listen.'

A deep, mournful bellowing was coming from the other side of the tree.

Aroo! Aroo! Aroooo!

Jamie and Tom whirled round. An enormous beaky head loomed out of the mist. The baby began squeaking excitedly.

'That must be the baby's mother,' Tom said.

The huge ankylosaurus lumbered slowly towards them.

'Awesome!' Jamie gasped. 'She's as big as a tank. And look at the size of that club at the end of her tail!'

The mum anky stopped. She stared at Jamie, Tom, and Wanna. Then she began to beat her clubbed tail into the marsh, sending up plumes of muddy spray.

'Uh oh,' Jamie whispered. 'She doesn't like us.'

Aroooomph! she snorted.

Wanna tried to hide behind

Jamie.

'She's going to charge us!'

Tom yelled.

'**Run!**'

The boys and Wanna darted behind
the twisted tree trunk.

'What's happening?' Tom asked.

Jamie peered out.

'She's not charging! She must
know she'll get stuck if she comes any

closer.' He looked over to the baby anky. It had stopped squealing and thumping its tail.

Maybe there is still a chance to help it, Jamie thought.

Tom crept out from the cover of the tree.

'The poor thing's stopped thrashing,' he said. 'It's exhausted!'

'We can get close to it now,' Jamie said. 'Perhaps we can push it out.'

'It's worth a try,' Tom agreed. 'As long as the mum will let us.'

The boys picked their way round to the back of the baby.

'OK,' said Jamie. 'The ground's solid here. Be careful not to step into the slime and watch out for that tail!

One, two, three . . . heave!'

They pushed as hard as they could, but the baby dinosaur didn't budge.

Beneath the anky's armoured bottom, the swamp began to gloop and burble. There was a loud whooshing noise and the surface of the slime boiled.

Plop! *Plop! Plop!*

The bubbles burst, splattering their faces with gunge.

A hideous smell welled up around them. Jamie coughed and gagged. It was even worse than rotten eggs.

'What's that smell?' Tom gurgled.
His face was dripping with green slime.

'Anky gas!' Jamie gagged. 'It
farted!'

'I didn't know baby ankies had rocket boosters,' Tom gasped, fanning at the air.

'They'd be easier to get out of the bog if they did.' Jamie grimaced. 'One more try!'

The baby anky didn't move.

'It's like trying to push a truck,' Jamie groaned.

'That's what we need,' said Tom. 'A truck to pull it out of the swamp.'

'Or a tank . . . ' Jamie looked across at the mum ankylosaurus and thought hard. 'We might not have a truck or a tank,' he said, 'but we do have the next best thing.'

Tom grinned. 'You're right! Now all we need is some rope.'

The boys looked at each other.

'Creepers!' they yelled together, rushing back to the tree where Wanna was munching on marsh plants. He wagged his tail as they came up to him.

'No time to play,' Jamie told him. 'We're busy!'

Jamie and Tom heaved at the dangling creepers, but they didn't break off.

'It's good that they're strong,' Tom said. 'But we've got to get some down!'

'I'll climb up and cut some off.' Jamie shinned up a vine, straddled the branch, and rummaged in his backpack, pulling out the fossil belemnite. 'I knew this would come in useful,' he muttered and used the fossil's sharp point to hack away at the vines.

As the creepers fell to the ground, Jamie swung back down to Tom.

'We'll need to tie them together,' he told Tom.

'Do you know any good knots?'

Tom nodded. 'A fisherman's knot!' Tom showed Jamie how to do it.

Fig 1

Soon, they had three long lengths of vine. They twisted them together for strength, and made a big loop at each end.

Fig 2

'We'll need some treats,' Tom said. Wanna watched hopefully as the boys

Fig 3

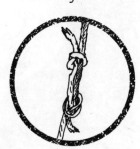

Fig 4

stuffed their pockets with the yellow marsh plant petals.

'Not for you,' Jamie told him. 'For the ankies.'

Wanna seemed a little disappointed.

'Now we've got to get these loops around the dinosaurs,' Jamie told Tom. The boys sloshed back to the baby anky and Tom dropped a flower for him to eat. Then Tom carefully threw his loop over the baby's head.

'That's the easy bit.' Jamie clutched the loop at the other end of the vines. 'Now for the mum . . .' He pulled a handful of petals from his pocket and slowly approached her.

75

The mum anky fixed
Jamie with her hooded
eyes and lowered her head.

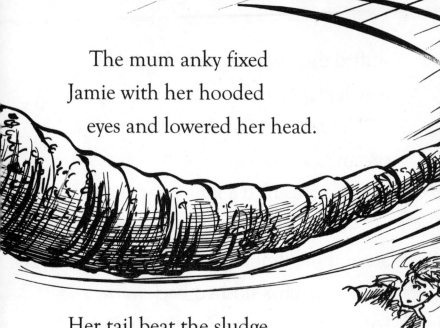

Her tail beat the sludge,
splattering him with stagnant
water. Jamie threw a petal in front of
her. She sniffed at it and ate it.

'So far, so good,' Jamie murmured.
He crept closer and threw a whole
handful of petals to the side. She
twisted round to eat them.

'Watch out!'

Tom yelled.

Jamie jumped out of the way as
the club on the end of the mum's tail
whipped past his head.

'Throw more flowers!' Tom called.
'Turn her right round.'

Jamie flung more petals on the
marsh, moving around to keep out of
the way of the clubbed tail. The mum
anky turned and began to graze.
Jamie picked up the vine rope and
took hold of the loop.

He threw it, like a lasso, over her shoulders, but it snagged on one of the horns.

'Missed!' Jamie muttered. The anky carried on chewing peacefully on the petals.

'She hasn't noticed,' Tom called.

'I'll unhook it and try again!' Jamie crept towards her and took hold of the loop wedged behind her horn. He could feel the steam from her nostrils as he worked it free.

Suddenly the baby anky began to snort and wail.

Aroooph! The mum anky lifted her head, jerking Jamie off his feet.

His wrist was caught in the vines!

Aroop,

aroop,

aroop!

The mum anky stumbled into the bog, with Jamie dangling from her neck. He struggled to get loose as her tail thrashed angrily, but he was stuck. Then the two front legs of the huge beast began to sink into the pool of sludge.

I'm doomed, Jamie thought. *Like Grandad said, the mud will swallow me up and spit out my bones!*

 79

CHAPTER 6

Dangling just above the slime, Jamie realized that the safest place to be was on top of the dinosaur.

Pulling with all his might, he hauled himself up onto the back of the mum anky's neck. He untangled the loop

from the horn, then quickly
reached down over her head
and slipped it around her neck.

Tom was gawping at him.

Jamie gave Tom the thumbs up
sign and got unsteadily
to his feet. His muddy
trainers got a grip on the
anky's rough plating

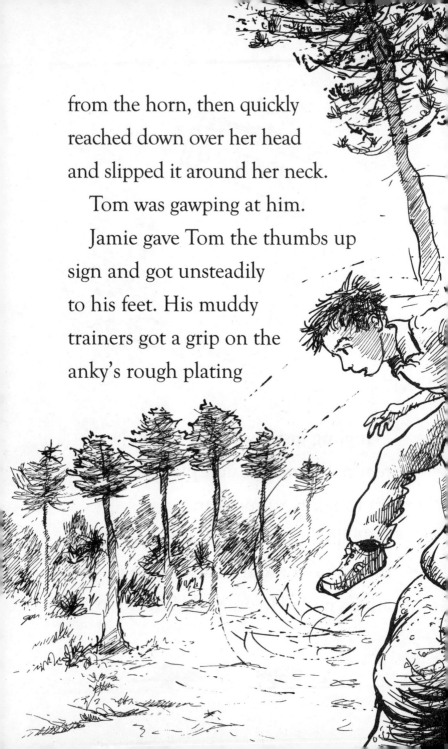

and he turned and ran along the
anky's thick neck and up over her
wide body between the two rows of
spikes. He sprang off her back and
landed next to Tom.

'Awesome!'
Tom grinned.
'You just ran over
a dinosaur!'

'Better than a dinosaur
running over me,' Jamie
said. 'Now all we've got to do
is turn her round again and
get her to pull her baby out.
We'll need lots of petals
for that!'

The boys gathered armfuls of the
juiciest looking marsh plants.

'Here, Anky!' Jamie threw some
plants just out of reach of the
mum ankylosaurus.

The great beast lifted her front legs out of the sludge, moved slowly towards them and began to chew.

'More!' Tom threw more petals in front of her. As the mum strained towards them, the length of vine attaching her to her baby tightened.

'It's working!' Tom cheered as the mum anky lurched forward onto dry land heaving her baby out after her. The baby struggled to its feet.

'Yes!' Jamie and Tom leaped into the air to give each other a high five as the mum anky turned and touched beaks with her baby.

'We'd better take off the vines,' Jamie said.

'My turn!' Tom grinned. 'You keep them busy eating.'

Wanna bounded up, wagging his tail. He dropped a mouthful of petals at Jamie's feet.

'Thanks, Wanna, that's just what we need.' Jamie threw petals in front of the ankies' beaks. As they munched, Tom carefully unhitched the vines from their necks and slowly backed away.

The ankies stopped eating. They raised their heads together and made a soft high-pitched arooping noise.

'I think they're saying thank you!'
Jamie said in amazement.

As Jamie, Tom, and Wanna
watched, the mist thinned.

The mum gently nudged her
baby and they turned away from
the boys. Ahead of them, a line of
ankylosaurs was marching slowly
onwards.

'It's the rest of their herd!' As
Jamie spoke, the mum and baby
lumbered over to the line calling
Aroop!

The herd stopped and turned their
heads. *Aroop! Aroop!* They lowed in
reply as mum and baby caught up
with them. The mum nudged her
baby between the legs of the biggest
ankylosaurus.

'That must be the dad,' Tom said.

The mum anky moved in behind
him as the herd of armoured beasts
continued its march.

Wanna grunked happily and
turned back towards the trackway.

'Our first dino rescue,' Jamie said

with satisfaction. 'But Wanna's right.
It's time to go home.'

'You should see yourself!' Tom
laughed as they trudged after Wanna.
'You're a sight!'

'Look who's talking!' Jamie

grinned. Tom was covered from head to toe in stinky green marsh mud.

They trekked up Gingko Hill and stopped by Wanna's nest.

'We have to go back now, Wanna,' Jamie told him. He took the last of the gingko fruit out of his backpack.

Grunk grunk. Wanna wagged his tail and settled down happily to chew his treat.

'See you next time!'

Jamie stepped backwards through the dinosaur footprints, feeling the ground turn to stone under his feet. He was back in the cave,

and a moment
later Tom stood
beside him.

Jamie shone his
torch on Tom. The
green slime that
had covered
him in Dino
World had
turned into a
thick layer of dust.

He sniffed at
the dust on his own
T-shirt.

'Yuck!' he sneezed. 'It

still stinks of marsh and anky
gas. We'd better get it off before
anyone notices.'

They squeezed back through the
gap and scrambled down
the boulders towards the beach.
The tide was out. In the distance,
Grandad waved and began to

pick up his fishing gear. Jamie
waved back.

'Beat you into the sea!' he
challenged Tom.

The boys raced across the beach,
threw themselves into the sea, and
came up spluttering.

'I was first,' laughed Jamie.

'No, I was first,' grinned Tom.

They splashed water all over each other until they were sure they'd washed off every trace of ankylosaurus.

'Ahoy there, me hearties,' Grandad greeted them as they emerged dripping from the sea. 'It looks as if you've had fun today!'

'Great fun!' Tom said. 'But I'd better be getting home now. See you tomorrow, Jamie?'

'You bet!' Jamie waved as Tom set off for the village.

'What have you boys been up to?' Grandad asked Jamie as they walked up towards the lighthouse.

 98

'We've been tracking dinosaurs!'
Jamie told him. 'But don't worry,
Grandad—we were careful. We didn't
get stuck in the mud.'

DINOSAUR WORLD

---- BOYS' ROUTE

Jungle

Misty
Lagoon

White
Ocean

100

Far Away Mountains

Crashing
Rock
Falls

Great
Plains

Fang
Rock

Gingko
Hill

GLOSSARY

Ankylosaurus (an-ki-low-sor-us) – a vegetarian dinosaur known for its armoured coat and clubbed tail (see below). Its armour consisted of large bony bumps similar to the covering of modern-day crocodiles and lizards.

Belemnite (bell-em-nite) – an extinct squid-like sea creature. Belemnite had ten arms of similar length with small hooks and beak-like mouths. Its fossils usually only preserve the creature's bullet-shaped body.

Bog – wetlands with soggy, spongy ground that are often too soft to walk across.

Clubbed tail – the tail of an ankylosaurus which resembled a huge, armoured golf club. The ankylosaurus used its tail as a weapon and could break bones of its enemies with a swift swing.

Fisherman's knot – named for its usefulness to fishermen. Two knots are tied in two ropes lying side by side. Tie a knot in one rope and slip the other rope through the hole; then tighten. Do the same to the other rope.

Fossil Finder – hand-held computer filled with dinosaur facts.

Gingko (gink-oh) – a tree native to China called a 'living fossil' because fossils of it have been found dating back millions of years, yet they are still around today. Also known as the stink bomb tree because of its smelly apricot-like fruit.

Marsh – shallow wetlands that are almost continuously flooded by a variety of sources, including rain, streams, and the sea.

Predator – an animal that hunts and eats other animals.

Wannanosaurus (wah-nan-oh-sor-us) – a dinosaur that only ate plants and used its hard, flat skull to defend itself. Named after the place it was discovered: Wannano in China.

Look up!
It'll be there
in soon...

Turn the page
to read the
first chapter of the
next adventure in the

Dinosaur Cove™

series:

Flight of the
Winged Serpent

'This exhibit looks so cool!'
exclaimed Jamie, as his best friend
Tom glued on the last miniature
jungle tree.

The two boys had spent the
morning painting the prehistoric

landscape and were just finishing the scenery. The scale model was as big as the table top and was going to be one of the exhibits in Jamie's dad's new dinosaur museum on the bottom floor of the old lighthouse where they lived.

'The marsh is my favourite,' Tom said, putting down the glue.

The model was labelled 'Late
Cretaceous Period' and had a jungle,
a plain, a beach with cliffs, and an
eerie-looking marsh. Dad had set
up a smoke machine under the table
so that smoke blew over the marsh
like mist.

Dad walked into the room
with the post. 'You two

have done a brilliant job painting the ocean,' he told them, and grinned at their paint-splattered clothes. 'And yourselves!'

Next, Jamie and Tom added the most important items to the display— the dinosaurs! They arranged a herd of triceratops on the green plain.

'They're just right there,' said Dad. 'They look as if they're grazing.' He stuck his head into a crate and started rummaging. Sawdust flew everywhere. 'Can't find the edmontosaurus,' came his muffled voice. 'I'm sure they're in here somewhere.'

'Dad's models are great,' whispered Jamie, 'but they're not as good as the real thing.'

Jamie and Tom had a secret. They had discovered the entrance to an amazing land of living dinosaurs, and they visited it whenever they could.

Jamie picked up a tyrannosaurus rex and made it run across the plain towards an ankylosaurus with a roar.

Tom snatched up the ankylosaurus.

'Not such an easy meal, you bully!' He swung the tiny anky's clubbed tail at the t-rex.

'Whoops!' Tom gasped as the t-rex went flying out of Jamie's hand towards a shelf full of model creatures.

WHACK!

The t-rex crashed into a large winged creature which wobbled and fell.

Jamie dived like a goalie and caught it before it hit the floor.

'Good catch!' gasped Tom.

Jamie's dad came running over.

'Sorry, Mr Morgan,' said Tom. 'Is it broken?'

Jamie's dad checked the model's wings. 'No damage done,' he told them. 'Now, where should this go on the display?'

Jamie looked at the long beak, the outstretched wings, and bony crest on the head. 'It's a sort of pterosaur, isn't it?'

'Yes, it's a quetzalcoatlus. Here's its label.'

'*Ket-sal-kow-at-lus*,' Jamie read. 'That's a mouthful.'

'One of the biggest flying reptiles,' Dad explained. 'It had a twelve metre wingspan.'

'That's more than six Dads lying head to toe.' Jamie flung his arms out wide.

'What a monster!' Tom said.

'One thing we don't know is where these quetzies nested,' said Dad. 'On the marsh, on the beach, or in the jungle.' He put the quetzy back on the shelf. 'Here's a quest for you, boys. Do some research and help me decide where on the model to put it. That'll keep you out of trouble.'

Jamie and Tom grinned at each other. They knew exactly where to find out where the quetzalcoatlus nested—Dino World!

Jamie scooped up his backpack and charged after Tom down the rocky

steps from the lighthouse.
They raced across the
pebbly beach, whooping
with excitement, to the
steep headland path.

Clambering over the
mossy boulders they
were soon at the old
smugglers' cave—and
the entrance to their
secret world.

Tom slipped inside
with Jamie close behind.
They squeezed through
the tiny opening to
the second chamber.
Jamie shone his torch
over the rock floor.

'Here are the
footprints,' he said.
'Let's go!'

One step at a time, Jamie and Tom followed the fossilized dinosaur tracks that led to the wall at the back of the cave. One . . . two . . . The familiar crack of light appeared in the wall . . . three . . . four . . . The crack widened . . . Five!

When Jamie opened his eyes, the ground was spongy under his feet. Jamie and Tom were in Dino World again!

Jamie stepped out of the cave and squinted in the bright sunlight. He breathed in the hot, damp air. 'Awesome!'

A bristly tongue licked his hand. A little dinosaur with greenish brown markings stood looking up hopefully at him.

'It's Wanna!' he cried.

Tom gave the wannanosaurus a welcoming pat on his hard, flat head. Wanna wagged his tail happily and stuck out his tongue to investigate a blue spot on Jamie's shorts.

Grunk! Wanna spat.

'Paint tastes horrible, doesn't it, Wanna?' said Jamie.

'Let's find you some nice, stinky gingkoes to make it better.' He reached up and picked a handful of sticky orange fruits from a nearby gingko tree.

Wanna gulped down the gingkoes in one go, juice spilling out of his mouth and down his chest. His long, bristly tongue licked his face and he grunked happily.

Jamie stuck a few more gingkoes in his backpack.

The boys went to the edge of the steep slope that led down to the jungle. They scanned the thick green canopy of trees below.

'One thing's for sure,' said Tom, 'quetzies couldn't live in there—not with that huge wingspan. The trees are too close together. And I don't see any nests in the tree tops.'

Jamie opened his Fossil Finder and put quetzalcoatlus in the search.

'*THOUGHT TO HAVE EATEN LIKE HERON, DIVING DOWN FOR FISH*,' he read. 'So maybe they live near water.'

'Misty Lagoon?' said Tom. 'But I only remember seeing smaller pterosaurs there—nothing as big as a quetzy.'

'How about White Ocean?' said Jamie eagerly. He shielded his eyes with his hand and peered out over the jungle, to where the ocean waves broke in a white line.

Tom whipped his compass out of his pocket. 'West it is.'

Join Jamie and Tom in **Dino World** with the

Dinosaur Cove™

CRETACEOUS SURVIVAL GUIDE

Turn the page for a taster of all the **awesome** things to do . . .

Create!

MAKE YOUR OWN EDIBLE DINO POO!

YOU WILL NEED:

- 100g plain chocolate
- 50g margarine
- 2 tablespoons golden syrup
- 150g plain digestive biscuits

Don't forget to ask a grown-up to help melt the chocolate!

1 Put the biscuits in a large freezer bag and tie the bag shut. Using a rolling pin, bash the biscuits into crumbs.

2 Break up the chocolate into pieces and put them in a saucepan. Heat the pan on a low temperature until the chocolate has melted.

3 Stir the margarine and syrup into the melted chocolate.

4 Take the saucepan off the heat. Pour the biscuit crumbs into the chocolate mixture and stir together.

36   37

Play!

WHICH CRETACEOUS DINO ARE YOU?

START

Do you walk on two legs or four legs?

Two legs — Four legs

Super speedy or supremely strong? — Speedy / Strong

Super speedy or supremely strong? — Strong / Speedy

Carnivore or herbivore? — Carnivore / Herbivore

Hunt on land or in the air? — Land / Air

Up high or down low? — Down low / Up high

Protected by horns or bony armour? — Horns / Bony armour

T-Rex   Quetzalcoatlus   Velociraptor   Wannanosaurus

Bagaceratops   Edmontosaurus   Triceratops   Ankylosaurus

Discover!

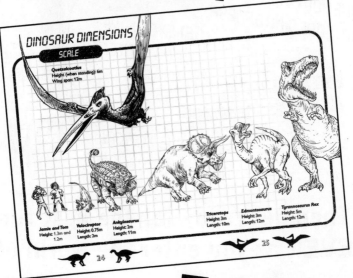

DINOSAUR DIMENSIONS

SCALE

Quetzalcoatlus
Height (when standing): 6m
Wing span: 12m

Jamie and Tom
Height: 1.3m and 1.2m

Velociraptor
Height: 0.75m
Length: 2m

Ankylosaurus
Height: 2m
Length: 11m

Triceratops
Height: 3m
Length: 10m

Edmontosaurus
Height: 3m
Length: 12m

Tyrannosaurus Rex
Height: 5m
Length: 12m

Explore!

T-REX: THE LIZARD KING

Tyrannosaurus Rex was a carnivore that ate all sorts of other creatures, from small dinosaurs like velociraptors to large ones like edmontosaurs. Palaeontologists think the t-rex was probably a scavenger as well as a hunter, eating up the remains of creatures that had already died. With chisel-shaped teeth at the front and huge teeth with knife-like serrated edges filling the rest of its mouth, the t-rex was a fearsome predator. The biggest t-rex skull ever found is 150cm long and was discovered in the 1960s. The biggest and best preserved whole t-rex skeleton is in the Field Museum of Natural History in Chicago. Its name is FMNH PR 2081, but its nickname is Sue.

We found out that competition for food was fierce in the Cretaceous period when we ran into not one but two t-rexes! We'd only just managed to escape one dino's snapping jaws when we stumbled into a battle between two of the massive lizard kings.